HELEN KELLER

BY ANNE SCHRAFF

Development: Kent Publishing Services, Inc.

Design and Production: Signature Design Group, Inc.

SADDLEBACK EDUCATIONAL PUBLISHING

Three Watson

Irvine, CA 92618-2767

Web site: www.sdlback.com

Photo Credits: page 33, Library of Congress; page 45, Zuma Press; page 51, Hulton Archive/Getty Images

Copyright © 2008 by Saddleback Educational Publishing.

All rights reserved. No part of this book may be reproduced in any form or by any means, electronic or mechanical including photocopying, recording, or any information storage and retrieval system, without the written permission of the publisher.

ISBN-13: 978-1-59905-249-6

ISBN-10: 1-59905-249-0

eBook: 978-1-60291-610-4

Printed in China

1 2 3 4 5 6 10 09 08 07

TABLE of CONTENTS

Chapter 1	4
Chapter 2	10
Chapter 3	18
Chapter 4	24
Chapter 5	30
Chapter 6	36
Chapter 7	42
Chapter 8	48
Chapter 9	55
Chapter 10	59
Bibliography	62
Glossary	63
Index	64

CHAPTER 1

When Helen Keller fell ill with a terrible fever as a toddler, she was left blind and deaf. Most people had little hope that Helen would have a productive life. With such a severe disability, she would surely live her life in the shadows.

But, Helen reached out for education and a full life. In doing so, she forever changed the way disabled people are seen. Helen was a **trailblazer**. She showed America and the world that physical disabilities were less important than a courageous heart and spirit.

Helen Adams Keller was born on June 27, 1880. She was born in Tuscumbia, Alabama, a small country town. Her father, Arthur Henley Keller, was a **veteran** of the Civil War. He was a captain in the southern **Confederacy**. He later became a cotton plantation owner and editor of the local newspaper, the *Alabamian*.

Arthur Keller was a widower with two sons when he married Kate Adams. She was twenty years younger than him. Tall, blue-eyed Kate Adams helped her husband run the plantation. To **supplement** the family finances, she made her own butter, lard, bacon, and ham.

The Kellers lived in a white house that was built fifty years earlier. Helen was the couple's first child. She was a bright, active baby, who spoke at six months of age. At a year old, she could walk.

When her mother was bathing her one day, Helen was **fascinated** by an object that was far away from her. She slid off her mother's lap and went running to get it. She learned to walk and run at an early age. Little Helen startled visitors by calling out words like "wah-wah" for water while still a baby.

In February 1882 when Helen was nineteen-months-old, she became sick and feverish. The fever worsened. Her parents feared she would die. At the time the illness was called "brain fever." It was probably either meningitis or scarlet fever.

Helen was desperately ill for several days. But the fever went away and she recovered. Helen's parents did not immediately realize the terrible thing that had happened to their daughter.

Gradually, there were frightening indications that she had lost her hearing and her sight. When the dinner bell rang, Helen did not respond. When her mother passed her hand in front of Helen's face, the child did not seem to notice. It was obvious that she was blind and deaf as a result of the illness.

Helen clung to her mother's skirts for the first few weeks after the illness. She spent most of her time in her mother's lap.

The only way Helen could make herself understood to her family was to shake her head for "no" and nod for "yes." She learned to act out her desires. If she wanted some buttered bread, she pretended she was cutting bread off the loaf and then buttering it.

Helen was a clever little girl. She soon learned to take the laundry from the basket and put it away neatly. She recognized her own **garments** from the rest. Sometimes, Helen touched her mother's lips and realized she was talking. But Helen could not hear what she was saying.

The little girl knew she was different because she did not talk. Helen tried moving her lips but since she could not hear, she did not make recognizable sounds.

Helen had periods of frustration about her disability. She kicked and screamed in wild **tantrums** until she was so tired she fell to the floor and slept. Relatives and friends were horrified at the girl's tantrums. Many believed she belonged in a hospital.

Helen did find one playmate who understood her very well. Martha Washington was the daughter of the Keller's black cook. Blonde Helen and dark-haired Martha played together constantly.

Joining the girls in their daily games was an old dog named Belle. Helen and Martha kneaded dough, made ice cream, cut out paper dolls, and climbed trees. They fed the hens and turkeys and hunted for eggs, which they brought in for breakfast. Martha could communicate with Helen better than anyone else.

CHAPTER 2

Helen Keller loved Christmas because she enjoyed picking over the raisins, grinding spices, and licking spoons. She also liked the wonderful kitchen smells.

One day, Helen spilled some water on her apron. She leaned close to the fire to dry the cloth. Soon, she was on fire. Her nurse threw a blanket over her. The blanket **stifled** the flames and saved her from serious injury.

Helen was a **mischievous** child, who once locked her mother in the pantry. She sat outside the locked door laughing as she felt the pounding of her mother's fist as she tried to escape.

When Helen was five, a sister, Mildred, was born. At first, Helen was jealous of the baby. Helen was the one usually sitting in her mother's lap. Now that spot was taken by Mildred.

Helen had a doll named Nancy. Nancy was plain looking and worn, but much loved by the little girl. Helen often put Nancy in the baby cradle once occupied by Helen herself. She loved to rock Nancy in the cradle.

One day, she was about to put Nancy in the cradle, when she found Mildred asleep in the it. Helen flew into a wild rage. She violently overturned the cradle, sending Mildred flying. Only quick action by the girls' mother saved Mildred from injury.

Helen's tantrums were growing more violent and troublesome as she grew older. Her parents suffered from her daily outbursts. No family meal could be eaten in peace. The little girl ran from place to place grabbing food and yelling.

Helen's parents were desperate for some way to help Helen and restore peace to the family. They could not bear the smashed dishes and lamps and the fierce screams anymore.

There were no specialists in blind and deaf children in little Tuscumbia. So, Helen's parents knew they had to look elsewhere.

Helen's mother had just read a book by Charles Dickens called *American Notes.* One chapter described progress made by an **oculist** from Baltimore, Maryland. He was working with a child who was blind and deaf like Helen.

Kate Keller was filled with hope that the oculist might be able to help Helen too. She headed for Baltimore with Helen.

Six-year-old Helen loved riding on the train. She was so thrilled by all the new experiences that she did not even have any tantrums. The other passengers were touched and amused by the lively little blonde girl who hurried up and down the aisles. Helen made friends with everybody in the railroad car.

The Baltimore oculist examined Helen and **concluded** that she could not be helped by surgery. But, he thought she could be taught to read and write. He suggested she be taken to an expert in the problems of deaf children. The expert was Alexander Graham Bell, the inventor of the telephone.

Bell had a lifelong interest in the deaf. His father had discovered methods of helping deaf people. He passed his interest on to his son. At this time, Bell felt that his most important work was in helping the deaf.

Bell met Helen and her mother. He suggested that they contact Michael Anagnos, director of the Perkins Institution. Bell thought Anagnos could recommend a good teacher for Helen.

The Kellers visited Anagnos. He suggested as Helen's teacher a twenty-one-year-old woman who had graduated from the Perkins Institution —Anne Sullivan.

Anne Sullivan was born in 1866 in Feeding Hills, Massachusetts. Her parents were Irish immigrants who could not read or write. At age 5, Anne **contracted** trachoma, a serious eye disease. The disease left her almost blind. She could only see blurry colors.

Anne's mother died of tuberculosis and her father left. Ten year old Anne and her brother, Jimmie, were sent to a **poorhouse**. Jimmie then died of tuberculosis. But, at age fourteen, Anne was sent to Perkins Institution. An eye operation there permitted her to read.

Anne Sullivan found it difficult to find regular work. When Michael Anagnos told her about Helen Keller, she jumped at the job offer. Anne had never taught before, but she was sure she could help the little girl.

On March 3, 1887, when Helen was almost seven-years-old, she met Anne Sullivan. Helen knew that someone was coming to teach her. She was very excited.

Helen **detected** the sense of expectation at the house. When Sullivan appeared in the yard, Helen ran to her. She flung herself at the young woman with such force that Sullivan almost fell over backwards.

Helen immediately began feeling Anne Sullivan's face, dress, and bag. Sullivan was surprised by the strength of the child.

Sullivan gave Helen a doll and she played with it for a while. Sullivan took Helen's hand and spelled the letters d-o-l-l into the palm of her hand. Helen repeated the finger movements on her own palm, but she did not understand what it all meant. Helen soon became frustrated. She hurled the doll to the ground.

Anne Sullivan knew she had to **discipline** Helen if she was going to teach her anything. Helen's parents felt sorry for their blind and deaf daughter. They always gave in to her every demand. Helen was a **willful** and disobedient child as a result.

Anne Sullivan wanted to tame Helen without breaking her strong spirit. She realized she had a great task before her.

CHAPTER 3

Helen refused to use utensils to eat. She preferred to use her fingers. She also had the habit of running around the table snatching food from other peoples' dishes. Her parents let her get away with this to avoid her tantrums.

Anne Sullivan refused to let her grab food from her plate. Helen threw herself on the floor and kicked and screamed for half an hour. Then, she tried to pull Sullivan's chair out from under her.

Finally, Helen pinched Sullivan who slapped her.

It hurt Helen's parents to see their blind and deaf child punished this way. But, it was the only way to make change.

It was decided that Anne Sullivan and Helen would move into the small garden house behind the main house. This would help Helen bond with her teacher. Also, it would spare the loving parents the sight of any necessary discipline.

Sullivan told Helen that she would have to learn to brush her own hair and button her shoes. Her mother would not be doing these things for her anymore. Helen screamed and kicked.

The one thing that Helen did enjoy was when Sullivan wrote words in the palm of her hand. So, every time Helen had a tantrum, Sullivan stopped writing in her hand. This was a serious punishment.

Little by little, Helen's behavior improved. Sullivan wrote more words into her hand. Although Helen still did not know what they all meant, she liked it. It was more communication than she had ever had with anyone.

One day, April 5, 1887, Helen and Anne Sullivan walked down to the water pump. Helen loved to go there because the smell of the honeysuckle vines was so sweet.

Up until this point, the words spelled into Helen's hand were a mysterious game. She enjoyed the game, but did not understand. She had no idea the words stood for things. She did not know that when the words were strung together, they made sentences and language.

Sullivan took Helen's hand and held it under the water spout. She let the water splash on her. On Helen's other hand, Sullivan spelled the word w-a-t-e-r on the child's palm.

Anne Sullivan saw an expression on Helen's face that she had never seen before. Helen looked thrilled. She had finally made the connection between the letters spelled into her hand and something real—water.

Helen's realization was called a miracle. Later on, Anne Sullivan would be called a miracle worker for breaking into the little girl's dark world and bringing the light of knowledge.

Helen was very excited by the discovery. She began racing around touching other objects and asking Sullivan to spell their names onto her palm. She wanted the names of the water pump and the trellis holding the honeysuckle vine spelled into her hand.

Everything she touched she demanded to know its name. Finally, Helen turned to Anne Sullivan and asked for her name. Sullivan took Helen's hand and spelled the word "teacher" on her palm.

In the next few hours, Helen learned the spelling of thirty new words. In just one month after coming to the Keller home, Sullivan had achieved a major breakthrough. A wall between Helen Keller and the world had been torn down. She would now soak up knowledge like a sponge, always eager for more.

The more Helen learned, the happier she became. Her progress was amazing. Her behavior problems improved dramatically as the world opened up for her.

Five days after the water pump incident, word of Helen's progress reached Michael Anagnos. He was delighted. He was proud of Sullivan's success and Helen's growth. Anagnos spread the word of the amazing little girl. Helen had benefited very much from the teaching of a graduate of Perkins Institution.

Anne Sullivan began teaching Helen to read. She used letters that were raised off of the page. Then, she used the Braille system of raised dots that represent letters of the alphabet. She taught Helen to write using what was called "square hand." Square hand uses letters with straight lines and no curves. Helen was able to write a short letter to her mother.

CHAPTER 4

When Helen Keller was only ten, there were photographs of her reading Shakespeare and playing with her dog in newspapers. Michael Anagnos was making her famous with articles about her progress. Anne Sullivan took Helen to visit Alexander Graham Bell and President Grover Cleveland at the White House.

In 1890 Helen lived at Perkins Institution during the school year. Anne Sullivan went with her to continue her special education. Helen loved the school because she was among children like herself who were blind and deaf. Before, she had been the only different one. But now she made friends with others like her and felt totally accepted.

When Helen came home to Alabama, she was polite and delightful. Her parents enjoyed her. She could talk to them with her fingers. But, Helen had a powerful desire to be able to talk with her voice.

There was nothing wrong with her vocal chords. She laughed and cried normally. But she became deaf before she was old enough to hear speech and understand it. Because of that, she could not speak in a normal voice.

Helen began working with teachers by touching their lips and throat as they spoke. She imitated the movement, but her voice did not come out right. Still, she continued to try to speak.

When she was 11, Helen Keller wrote a fairy story titled "The Frost King." She sent it to Michael Anagnos as a birthday gift to him. She loved him very much for all that he had done for her.

Anagnos was thrilled when he read the story. He published it in a Perkins magazine as evidence of what a deaf and blind child could achieve. Sadly, Helen thought the story was original. But she had a similar story spelled into her hand years earlier. That story was "The Frost Fairies," by Margaret Canby.

Apparently, Helen remembered the story, and large parts of her story were very similar to the earlier one. When this was discovered, Anagnos was angry. He believed he had been **deliberately** deceived. His friendship with Helen Keller ended. This was heartbreaking for the little girl.

For a long time, Helen Keller did not trust her own thoughts. She was afraid to write other stories. She feared that they too were remembered words from someone else.

In 1894 14-year-old Helen Keller enrolled at the Wright-Humason School for the Deaf in New York City. Dr. Thomas Humason and John Wright encouraged Helen's hopes that she might learn to speak. Anne Sullivan came with her. She attended classes with Helen. Anne spelled into Helen's hand what the teachers were saying.

Helen worked hard at the school. She learned many new skills. She learned how to play checkers, and she went horseback riding. She even took part in a school play. But, as hard as she tried, she could not speak well enough so that strangers could understand her.

Helen then began dreaming of doing something no blind and deaf person had ever done before. She wanted to go to college. In 1896 Helen enrolled at the Cambridge School for Young Ladies with Anne Sullivan to prepare for college.

Helen was now using a Braille writer. She read from **embossed** books with raised letters. She could use both a regular typewriter and a Braille one.

By this time, Helen had done a great deal of reading. She read histories about Greece, Rome, and the United States. She learned some French and Latin grammar. But many people still doubted that she could handle college work, even with Anne Sullivan's help.

Helen had made up her mind, however. She was going to enroll at Radcliffe College for Women, the companion school to Harvard University. At the time, Harvard only admitted men.

Helen Keller and Anne Sullivan arrived at Radcliffe College in 1900. They roomed off campus in a rental house. It would be a monumental struggle for Helen. It would also be a challenge for Anne Sullivan, whose own eyesight was impaired.

CHAPTER 5

Helen Keller had great dreams about college life. But, she never realized how difficult it would be for her to **absorb** so much material.

Keller and Sullivan rode to school every day on a **tandem bicycle**. They sat next to one another in class. Sullivan spelled into Keller's hand as much of the lecture as she could.

Then, at night, Helen Keller typed what she remembered on her Braille typewriter. She studied from those notes. Keller was often frustrated, but she worked hard. When freshman exams came, she passed in all her subjects. Those subjects were French, German, history, English composition, and English literature.

Helen Keller's political ideas began to take form. As a teenager, she had visited the slums of New York. She noticed the terrible smells and learned about the poor, terrible lives of the people there.

She thought it was unfair that anybody should live like this. Keller began to think there was something wrong with the political system of the country. Some people were very rich, and others had almost nothing.

At the beginning of her sophomore year at Radcliffe, Keller was called from class one day. A man named William

Alexander wanted to talk to her about writing articles about her life. He was the editor of a popular magazine, the *Ladies Home Journal.*

Helen Keller's experience in college was a great human interest story. Keller was offered three thousand dollars for the articles, a large sum of money.

At first, Keller was not sure she had the time to write the articles with the demands of her college work. But John Macy, a twenty-five-year-old English literature teacher at Harvard, helped her organize her thoughts. The articles appeared in the magazine. Helen Keller was proud and thrilled.

John Macy then **promoted** the articles as a book. It was published as *The Story of My Life* in 1903. It was not a commercial success, but it became a classic book.

On June 28, 1904, Helen Keller graduated from Radcliffe College. She had earned a Bachelor of Arts (B.A.) degree. She graduated cum laude, or with honors. She became the first deaf and blind person to graduate from college with a B.A.

Portrait of Helen Keller

Helen Keller and Anne Sullivan went to live at Wrentham. It was a country village about an hour away from Boston, Massachusetts. Keller was not quite sure what her future held for her. She hoped she would be a writer.

Keller and Sullivan were very happy together. They traveled and shopped for nice clothing. Then John Macy fell in love with Anne Sullivan. He came often to the Wrentham house and helped with repairs. Finally, he asked Sullivan to marry him.

Sullivan was ten years older than Macy, but she loved him. She **hesitated** in accepting his proposal. She worried about Helen. When Helen learned of Sullivan's doubts, she gave her full blessing to the marriage. On May 2, 1905, in the flower-filled living room of the Wrentham house, the pair was married. Keller was a joyous witness.

After Anne and John Macy returned from their honeymoon, they moved into the Wrentham house. They lived there with Helen Keller. The three became a close knit family.

Helen loved John like an older brother. They took long walks together. They sometimes played chess and talked politics. John Macy was progressive in his politics, leaning toward **socialism**. Helen agreed with that, but Anne was more conservative.

Household chores were divided between the two women. Anne did the cooking and gardening. Helen cleared the table, did the dishes, and made the beds. Helen Keller and John Macy dreamed of having great writing careers. All Anne Sullivan Macy wanted was a baby.

CHAPTER 6

In 1909 Helen Keller published *The World I Live In*. It described her everyday life. She began to get mail from all over the world from people who read her books.

John Macy and Helen Keller joined the Socialist party. Keller was offended by the luxury of the wealthy and the ten-hour work days of ordinary people. The Socialists believed everyone should have the same living standard. Anne

Sullivan did not agree with Helen and John's political ideas.

Keller criticized rich men like John D. Rockefeller and Andrew Carnegie who had personal fortunes. Then Andrew Carnegie, who gave a lot to charitable causes, offered Keller an income.

Carnegie offered Keller five thousand dollars a year. He felt that her courage was making an outstanding **contribution** to society. Keller politely turned the money down, even though she could have used it. She could not accept it from a rich man.

Keller hung a large red flag from her bedroom window to show her support for socialism. Many of her friends were upset. They thought Keller did not really understand politics. They felt that the Socialists were using her.

Keller found out people were saying she was not able to understand complicated economic ideas. She struck back. She said she felt insulted that anyone disrespected her like that. She said being blind and deaf had nothing to do with her mind.

Keller and Anne and John Macy were having economic problems. None of the trio had a job that paid well. The decision was made to have a lecture tour. The tour would feature Helen Keller as a way to raise money. But, first Keller had an operation on her eyes.

One of her eyes **jutted** out. That was why she was always photographed in **profile**. The purpose of the operation was to remove her sightless eyes and replace them with artificial eyes. This would give her a more pleasing appearance.

In February 1913 Keller made her first appearance in an auditorium in Montclair, New Jersey. She was terrified to go before the public. She prayed for strength.

Anne Macy spoke first for about an hour, telling Keller's story. Then, Helen came out and placed her fingers on Anne's mouth. This showed the audience the skill of lip reading. Then, Helen Keller gave a short talk.

Her comments were filled with hope and good will, but her voice was of poor quality. It was high pitched and odd. The final part of the presentation was a question and answer period. The entire presentation lasted about two hours.

The lecture tours supported Keller for a while. But then Anne's vision grew worse. Sadly, her marriage to John Macy ended in 1914. This left Anne very depressed. Anne could not help Helen on the stage. So, a new assistant—Polly Thomson—was hired.

With Thomson assisting, Keller continued to **draw** large crowds. Thomas Edison and former President Howard Taft came to see Keller. The famous Italian tenor, Enrico Caruso, sang to Helen. Auto pioneer Henry Ford invited her to tour the Detroit factory where he was building automobiles.

World War I had broken out in Europe. Helen Keller joined women's peace groups. The groups campaigned against American involvement in the war.

Keller made some **controversial** remarks against war and **capitalism**. She called John D. Rockefeller a monster. She blasted President

Theodore Roosevelt as bloodthirsty. She said this because he wanted the United States to join World War I.

Keller was warned by friends that she could not continue to make such statements. People might consider her unpatriotic. Keller then said she would gladly go to jail for her beliefs if it came to that.

In 1916, Keller joined the National Woman's Party. This was a **militant** group campaigning for giving women the right to vote. Keller believed in that strongly. Keller also continued to speak out boldly in favor of socialism. She also still spoke out against American participation in World War I.

CHAPTER 7

In 1916 Helen Keller became friends with a twenty-nine-year-old Socialist named Peter Fagan. He helped her with her lecture tour.

But then, Anne Sullivan fell ill. Polly Thomson took her to a **sanitarium**. Helen was alone. She had no choice except to return to Alabama and live with her mother.

Peter Fagan followed Keller to Alabama. They took walks together. He held Helen's hand. Finally, he told her that he loved her and wanted to marry her. Keller was seven years older than Fagan, but she loved him too. She was overjoyed.

Fagan learned to read Braille. As he and Keller walked in the woods, he spelled words to her. Helen Keller's mother was very upset when she learned that Helen and Peter were planning their wedding.

Kate Keller, Helen's mother, ordered Fagan out of Helen's life. Helen's mother believed someone like her daughter should not marry anyone. Fagan repeatedly came to the house in Alabama to see Helen. Finally, at Kate Keller's request, family members forced him away at gun point.

Helen Keller continued to hope for Fagan's return. But, when she finally gave up, she looked at her brief romance as a beautiful part of her life.

Helen Keller was very unhappy in Alabama. She felt like a prisoner. She desperately missed Anne Sullivan and Polly Thomson. She felt useful and alive when she was with them.

In 1917 Anne Sullivan was feeling better. Helen and Polly came to join her. They lived in a red brick cottage in Forest Hills, New York. Keller's interest in the world around her returned.

The United States entered World War I. She continued to **grieve** about the U.S. involvement in the war.

She also became very aware of widespread discrimination against African Americans in the South. She remembered little Martha Washington who she had played with as a child. She felt black children, like Martha, should be completely equal to white children.

Keller's opposition to racial segregation was shocking to her Alabama relatives. But, Helen did not care what other people thought.

Helen, Anne, and Polly were happy living together in New York. Then, an offer came their way from Hollywood, California. A producer wanted to make Keller's life into a movie.

Helen Keller and Polly Thompson

He was offering Keller and Sullivan ten thousand dollars each if they signed the contract. When the movie was finished, they would each get another ten thousand. After that they might get royalties. It sounded wonderful.

Keller traveled by train to California and took part in some scenes in the movie when her older years were covered. The movie, *Deliverance,* did not turn out to be a commercial success. In the end, it did not provide the economic security they had hoped for.

In 1920 Helen Keller turned forty. She was again in search of a source of income. The popularity of the lecture tour was **waning**. People suggested that Helen and her friends develop a **vaudeville** act and tour the country with it.

The idea of traveling around with acrobats, magicians, and animal acts did not **appeal** to Anne Sullivan. She saw vaudeville as undignified and a poor choice for Helen Keller's future. But, Keller was open to the idea.

A twenty minute act was developed for Helen Keller and Anne Sullivan. On February 24, 1920, the act opened at the Palace Theatre in Manhattan.

Anne was seated at a grand piano as the curtain parted. She spoke to the audience in her warm Irish-accented voice. She briefly told them Helen's story. Then a tall, slim, attractive Helen Keller appeared. They acted out the water pump incident. The act ended with Helen Keller, in her very limited voice, saying she once was **dumb**, but she is no more.

CHAPTER 8

Helen Keller's vaudeville act went to Baltimore, Pittsburgh, and many smaller cities. Anne Sullivan remained unhappy about it. But she was **steadfast** at Helen's side.

Kate Keller, Helen's mother, was horrified that her daughter had sunk to this level. But Helen Keller herself was having a great time. She felt part of a large, **vibrant** new group of people. They were fun and lively.

Keller rushed around making new friends and learning the amazing stories of interesting people. When Keller was not on stage herself, she enjoyed the other acts. She liked to be in the audience when the dancers came on. She could feel the boards beneath their whirling feet tremble. Helen clapped with the beat, a big smile on her face.

In November 1921 Kate Keller died. Helen had a strong religious belief in an afterlife. She felt that after people die they meet their loved ones in the great beyond. That **consoled** her in her loss.

In 1921 Robert Irwin founded the American Foundation for the Blind. He was blind and had a Master's degree. His organization had several goals.

One goal was to decide which was the best Braille system. Another was to increase the number of Braille books.

In 1923 Irwin contacted Helen Keller and asked her to become a fundraiser for the organization. At first, Keller did not like the idea. It sounded too much like the old stereotype of blind people begging for money. But Irwin convinced her that it was a very respectable thing to do.

Now done with vaudeville, Keller and Sullivan began addressing five meetings a week. They went to private homes asking for support for the foundation. Keller was told that her Socialist ideas might harm chances of getting donations for the blind. So, she agreed to abandon politics, at least for a while.

The team of Anne and Helen proved to be very popular. Keller's personality delighted people. In 1926 Keller met with President Calvin Coolidge. The president was generally regarded as an unfriendly person. He warmed to Keller, telling her she had a wonderful personality.

In 1929 Helen Keller's had a new book called *Midstream: My Later Life*. It was very successful. Keller began to testify before state legislatures and the United States Congress. She asked for more federal help in buying Braille books for the blind.

Helen Keller reading a book written in Braille

The three women, Helen, Anne, and Polly spent six months traveling through Britain, Scotland, and Ireland. Then, in the spring of 1931, the First International Conference for Workers for the Blind was held in New York. There were 31 nations represented. Helen Keller's fundraising efforts were praised.

Helen Keller was traveling more and more. She was seen as a symbol of an active, successful blind and deaf woman. Also, she was seen as a symbol of America. She always seemed cheerful and **optimistic**. Her clothing was attractive and eye catching. She wore a cute little hat with a fluffy, dotted veil. There were sparkling buckles on her shoes.

Helen Keller and her friends rented a villa in Brittany. From there, they traveled to other countries. While in Europe, Keller was saddened by the clouds of war that were gathering. She sensed the **hostility**. Once again, she spoke out for cooperation among nations.

When Helen Keller returned to the United States, she found out that an old friend was running for president. Much earlier, Keller had **corresponded** with New York Governor Franklin Roosevelt. The bond between them was deep.

Keller was encouraged that in 1932 Roosevelt would be running for the presidency. When he was elected president of the United States, Keller's friendship with him continued. He welcomed her input on assistance for the disabled.

Anne Sullivan's health had been declining for some time. She was the person who handled Keller's personal finances. Arrangements were made in case Sullivan died before Keller. If this happened, Helen Keller's finances would be handled by the Foundation for the Blind.

On October 20, 1936, Anne Sullivan suffered a heart attack and died. The funeral was held at the Presbyterian Collegiate Church in New York City. Helen Keller and Polly Thomson followed the **casket** down the aisle. Anne's body was **interred** in the National Cathedral in Washington. She was remembered as one of the greatest of all teachers.

CHAPTER 9

Helen Keller helped pass the bill providing for more Braille books. She helped President Roosevelt include assistance for the disabled in the new Social Security Act. Roosevelt said he was for whatever Keller was for.

Keller was becoming a national heroine. She was admired by Americans and people all over the world. She moved with Polly Thomson to Westport, Connecticut. They lived in a colonial house. There, they entertained many famous and non-famous people.

Helen Keller was sad that America was involved in another world war, World War II. But she understood the terrible evil of Hitler's Germany. She knew it had to be stopped.

She wanted to do her part in helping the war effort. So, she started visiting injured soldiers in hospitals. Keller's own disability was a great help in reaching out to severely disabled men, especially those blinded in the war.

In spite of her handicaps, she had become a beloved and successful woman. Her strength offered real encouragement to young men facing lifetime challenges. With Polly at her side, she was able to talk to the men.

Keller was now past sixty, but her active life continued. She campaigned for Franklin Roosevelt's reelection in 1944. She visited hospitals in London,

Paris, Athens, and Rome. She made these visits on behalf of the American Foundation for the Overseas Blind.

In 1947, after World War II, Keller visited Australia. She also returned to Japan where she had been so warmly received before. She visited institutions for the blind and spent time in Hiroshima. Hiroshima was one of the two Japanese cities that was bombed with atomic weapons.

Helen Keller pledged to work for peace. She wanted to help prevent atomic weapons from ever being used again. She spent 61 days in Japan and once again was received as a hero.

In 1950 Helen Keller visited South Africa. In 1952 she went to Israel, Egypt, Lebanon, Syria, and Jordan.

On the one hundredth anniversary of Louis Braille's death, Keller visited Paris.

Louis Braille was the man who developed the Braille system. Keller spoke about Braille's wonderful contribution in perfect French. She went on to India and Pakistan later. She never tired of her work as the unofficial ambassador of good will.

Helen Keller wrote a book titled *Teacher*. The book was about her much loved friend, Anne Sullivan.

On the week before her 75th birthday, Keller was awarded an honorary degree from Harvard University. It was the first ever given to a woman. Telegrams, gifts, and good wishes came to Keller from all over the world.

Polly Thomson had a stroke in 1957. She never was able to be Helen Keller's companion again. A nurse, Winnie Corbally, took over to help Keller at home.

CHAPTER 10

In 1957 a play was developed. It was based on the life of Helen Keller and the help Anne Sullivan had given her. The play was a great success as a live television play and then on the stage. Eventually the play, called *The Miracle Worker*, was made into a motion picture. Both Patty Duke, who played Helen, and Anne Bancroft, who played Anne Sullivan, won Academy Awards.

In 1960 Polly Thomson died. Her remains were placed in the National

BIBLIOGRAPHY

Keller, Helen. *The Story of My Life: A Restored Classic.* New York: W.W. Norton & Company, 1995.

Herrmann, Dorothy. *Helen Keller, A Life.* Chicago: University of Chicago Press, 1999.

GLOSSARY

absorb: to soak up

appeal: to be especially attractive

capitalism: an economic system

casket: a box in which a body is placed

conclude: to come to a conclusion or determination

Confederacy: the name of the Southern states of the United States that wanted to become a separate country during the Civil War

console: to calm someone down or make someone feel better

contract: to get or acquire

contribution: something that is donated or given

controversial: debatable; problematic

correspond: to belong to

deliberately: on purpose

detect: to notice

discipline: to teach manners and rules

draw: to attract

dumb: unable to speak

embossed: having a raised pattern

fascinated: to be very interested

garments: clothing

gradually: slowly

grieve: to mourn

hesitate: to pause

hostility: unfriendliness; aggression

inter: to bury

jut: to stick out

militant: engaging in aggression or war

mischievous: behaving in a slightly troublesome or naughty way

oculist: a doctor who treats eye diseases

optimistic: having a positive attitude

poorhouse: a place where poor people live

profile: a view from the side

promote: to encourage the advancement of something

sanitarium: an institution for the recovery of health

segregation: separation based on race, religion, or ethnicity a system of social and economic organization

steadfast: firm in purpose; unwavering

stifle: to end or put out

supplement: something added to complete something else

tandem bicycle: a bicycle for two people

tantrum: a fit of bad temper

trailblazer: a pioneer; someone who blazes a trail for others to follow

vaudeville: stage entertainment involving a series of short acts

veteran: someone who has experience in an occupation, particularly the military

vibrant: bright; glowing

waning: becoming smaller or weaker

willful: headstrong; stubborn

INDEX

Alexander, William, 31, 32
American Foundation for the Blind, 49, 50, 54
Anagnos, Michael, 4, 15, 23, 24
Baltimore, Maryland, 13
Bell, Alexander Graham, 14, 24
Braille, 23, 28, 30, 43, 49, 51, 55, 58
Braille, Louis, 57, 58
Carnegie, Andrew, 37
Cleveland, Grover, 24
Coolidge, Calvin, 50
Fagan, Peter, 42, 43
Feeding Hills, Massachusetts, 15
Ford, Henry, 40
Forest Hills, New York, 44
Harvard University, 29, 32
Hiroshima, 57
Humason, Thomas, 27
International Conference of Workers for the Blind, 52
Irwin, Robert, 49, 50
Keller, Arthur Henley, 5
Keller, Kate Adams, 5, 13, 43, 48, 49
Keller, Mildred, 11
Macy, John, 32, 34, 35, 36, 38, 39
meningitis, 6
National Woman's Party, 41
Perkins Institute, 14, 15, 23, 24, 26,

Radcliffe College for Women, 29, 31, 33
Roosevelt, Franklin, 53, 55, 56
scarlet fever, 6
Socialism, 41
Socialist, 36, 37, 42, 50
Sullivan, Anne, 14, 15, 16, 17, 18, 19, 20, 21, 22, 23, 24, 27, 28, 29, 30, 34, 35, 36, 38, 39, 40, 42, 44, 45, 46, 47, 48, 50, 53, 54, 58, 59, 60, 61
Sullivan, Jimmie, 15
the *Alabamian*, 5
Thomson, Polly, 40, 42, 44, 45, 52, 54, 55, 56, 58, 59, 61
tuberculosis, 15
Tuscumbia, Alabama, 5, 12
Washington, Martha, 9, 44, 45
Westport, Connecticut, 55
World War I, 40, 41, 44
World War II, 56, 57
Wrentham, Massachusetts 34, 35
Wright, John, 27
Wright-Humason School, 27